MAY -- 2021
STARK LIBRARY

DISCARD

THE MOON

BY ARNOLD RINGSTAD

Published by The Child's World®
1980 Lookout Drive • Mankato, MN 56003-1705
800-599-READ • www.childsworld.com

Photographs ©: JPL/USGS/NASA, cover, 1, 3, 13; NASA, 2, 18, 19, 22; Goddard/GSFC/NASA, 4, 9 (Sun), 9 (Moon); iStockphoto, 6; Bill Dunford/NASA, 7; NOAA/NASA, 8; JPL/NASA, 9 (Earth); JSC/NASA, 10, 12 (left), 14, 15; MSFC/NASA, 12 (right); Shutterstock Images, 16; Phitha Tanpairoj/Shutterstock Images, 20

Copyright © 2021 by The Child's World®
All rights reserved. No part of this book may be reproduced or utilized in any form or by any means without written permission from the publisher.

ISBN 9781503844735 (Reinforced Library Binding)
ISBN 9781503846173 (Portable Document Format)
ISBN 9781503847361 (Online Multi-user eBook)
LCCN 2019957918

Printed in the United States of America

About the Author

Arnold Ringstad loves reading about space science and exploration. He lives in Minnesota with his wife and their cat.

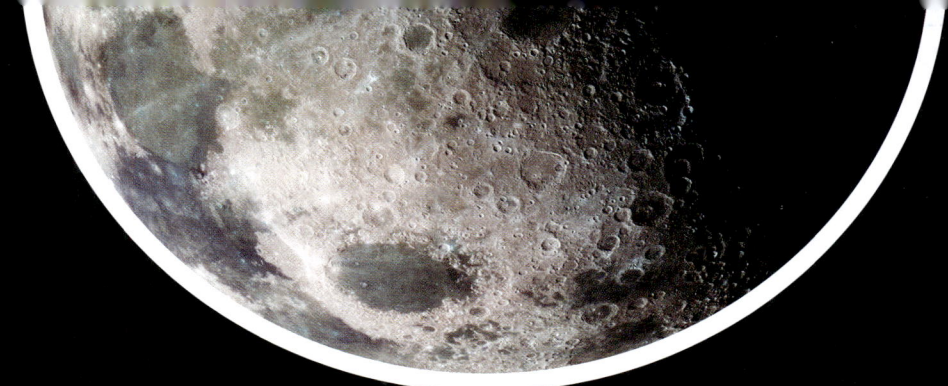

CONTENTS

CHAPTER ONE
EARTH'S NEIGHBOR IN SPACE . . . 5

CHAPTER TWO
WHAT IS IT LIKE ON THE MOON? . . . 11

CHAPTER THREE
EXPLORING THE MOON . . . 17

OUT OF THIS WORLD! . . . 22

GLOSSARY . . . 23

TO LEARN MORE . . . 24

INDEX . . . 24

▲ The Latin word for the moon is *Luna*. This is why we use the word *lunar* to talk about things related to the moon.

CHAPTER ONE

EARTH'S NEIGHBOR IN SPACE

The moon is Earth's closest neighbor in space. We can see it in the sky. It is the brightest thing in the night sky. Sometimes we can even see it during the day.

The moon is about 239,000 miles (385,000 km) from Earth. It **orbits** Earth. It takes about 27 days for the moon to circle the planet. We only see one side of the moon. The other side is always facing away.

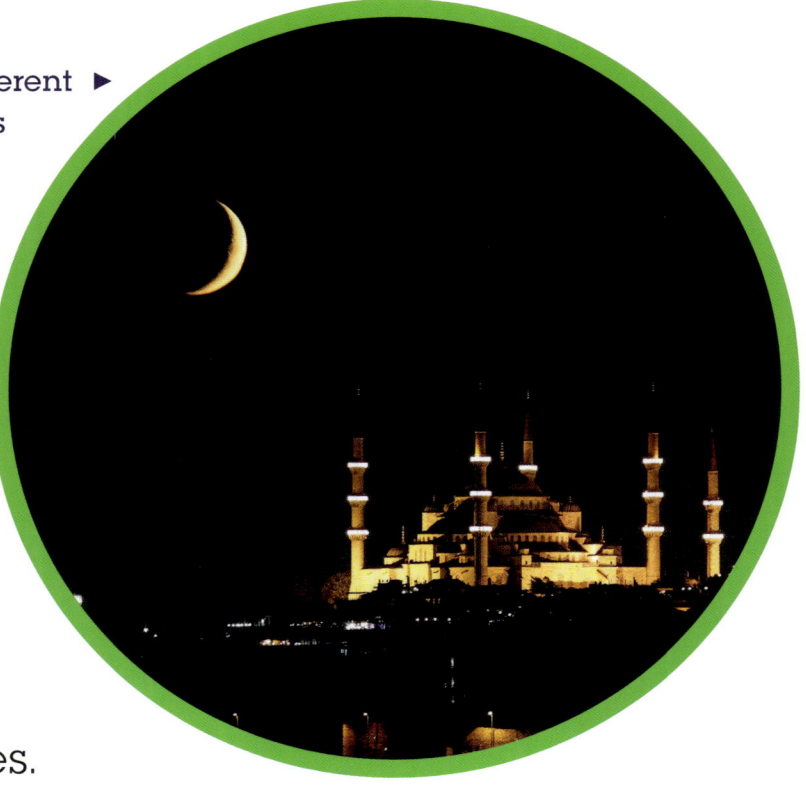

The moon is visible in different shapes. This picture shows a crescent moon over the Blue Mosque in Turkey.

However, the moon does not always look the same. The sun lights up different parts of it at different times. Sometimes the moon is a bright circle. Sometimes it is half bright and half dark. The moon may be a thin, curved shape called a crescent. And sometimes the moon is all dark. The sun is shining on the side we cannot see.

When the moon is becoming more visible, it's called *waxing*. When the moon is becoming less visible, it's called *waning*.

NEW	**WAXING CRESCENT**	**FIRST QUARTER**

WAXING GIBBOUS	**FULL**	**WANING GIBBOUS**

THIRD QUARTER	**WANING CRESCENT**	**NEW**

This image of the moon ▶ crossing between Earth and the sun was taken by NASA's Deep Space Climate Observatory (DSCOVR). The image shows the far side of the moon, which is not visible from Earth.

The moon is much smaller than Earth. Earth is 7,918 miles (12,742 km) across. The moon is just 2,159 miles (3,474 km) across. The larger an object is, the stronger its **gravity** is. The moon's gravity is weaker than Earth's. That means the same object would weigh less on the moon than on Earth. A 100-pound (45-kg) person would weigh just 16.6 pounds (7.5 kg) on the moon!

The moon's gravity has effects on Earth. It pulls on the water in the oceans. This creates **tides**. Tides are the rise and fall of water in the ocean. The sun's gravity helps create tides, too. But the moon is much closer. It has a bigger effect on tides.

DID YOU KNOW?

Sunlight shines on one side of Earth. It creates a shadow in space on the other side. Sometimes the moon moves into this shadow. This is called a lunar eclipse.

▲ Earth's atmosphere is visible in this picture taken from the International Space Station. Unlike Earth, the moon has almost no atmosphere.

CHAPTER TWO

WHAT IS IT LIKE ON THE MOON?

Earth has a thick **atmosphere**. It is made of gases. The gases help animals and plants survive. The gases also keep Earth at a comfortable temperature. The atmosphere protects Earth from **meteors**, too. These rocks from space fly toward the planet. The atmosphere slows them down before they hit the ground.

The moon is different. There is almost no atmosphere. That means there is nothing for people to breathe. The temperature is dangerous, too. It gets very hot and very cold. In sunlight, it can be 260 degrees Fahrenheit (127°C). In shadow, the temperature drops to −280 degrees Fahrenheit (−173°C). People need space suits or **spacecraft** to survive on the moon.

Without an atmosphere, the moon has nothing to slow down meteors. Space rocks have been hitting the moon for millions of years. The surface is covered in **craters**. These are holes dug when a meteor hits something. Some craters are huge. Other craters are tiny. These craters are formed when tiny grains of dust hit the moon.

These images were taken in 1969 ▶ during the Apollo 11 mission to the moon. They show the variety of craters on the moon's surface.
▼

DID YOU KNOW?

Tycho (TY-koh) is one easy-to-spot crater on the side of the moon facing Earth. It is about 52 miles (84 km) wide. There are many craters this size. But Tycho is easier to see because it is so new. Scientists believe it formed about 108 million years ago. Many other craters are almost four billion years old.

People left footprints in the moon's regolith dust when they walked on the moon's surface.

The rain of meteors has covered the moon in powdery dust. It is called lunar regolith. It gives the moon its light gray color. The moon has darker areas, too. These are known as seas, but they do not have water in them. Billions of years ago, lava flowed there. It cooled and made darker rock.

This image was taken from the Apollo 11 spacecraft in 1969. The area of the moon visible in the picture is called Smyth's Sea.

CHAPTER THREE

EXPLORING THE MOON

The moon sits in the night sky every night. That means people have looked at it for thousands of years. At first, they did not realize it was a place that could be visited. It was just a light in the sky. That changed in the 1600s. An Italian scientist named Galileo Galilei used a new invention called the telescope. The telescope made distant things look larger. Galileo looked at the moon. He studied the moon's craters, mountains, and plains. People realized they might someday walk on the moon. The hard part would be getting there.

◀ People looked at the moon for thousands of years before scientists learned how to travel to it.

Neil Armstrong took this photo of ▶ Buzz Aldrin on the moon in 1969.

In the 1950s, people made new kinds of **rockets**. These machines could blast off from Earth. They could zoom into space. They could even go all the way to the moon. People started using spacecraft to study the moon. Many spacecraft failed. But others succeeded. In 1959, the *Luna 3* spacecraft flew around the moon. It took pictures of the moon's far side. It was the first time people had seen that part of the moon.

Astronauts (left to right) Neil Armstrong, Michael Collins, and Buzz Aldrin ▶ had to stay away from people when they returned to Earth in case they brought back germs from the moon. President Richard Nixon (right) spoke to them during this time.

Moon exploration took another leap forward in 1969. In that year, the Apollo 11 mission flew to the moon. Three **astronauts** were on the mission. Two of them, Neil Armstrong and Buzz Aldrin, walked on the moon. The third astronaut was Michael Collins. He stayed in orbit around the moon.

DID YOU KNOW?

Putting the Apollo astronauts on the moon was a huge task. More than 400,000 men and women helped make it happen. They had many jobs. Everyone played an important role.

The astronauts took pictures of the moon. They collected regolith and rocks. The Apollo 11 astronauts returned home safely. Their work helped scientists learn a lot about the moon. Five more missions later landed on the moon. The last one was in 1972. Scientists continued to learn more.

No one has been to the moon since 1972. Some people want to change that. The U.S. government has started the Artemis program. It hopes to send people back to the moon by 2024. This would take new rockets and new spacecraft. Artemis missions would help us learn new things about our closest neighbor in space.

◀ Astronauts may visit the moon again someday with the Artemis program.

OUT OF THIS WORLD!
APOLLO 17

The last moon landing of the Apollo program was Apollo 17. The mission launched on December 7, 1972. It was the first night launch for an Apollo mission. The huge rocket lit up the sky as it left the ground.

Astronauts Eugene Cernan and Harrison Schmitt walked on the moon. Astronaut Ronald Evans waited in orbit around the moon. Cernan and Schmitt brought more science experiments than the earlier Apollo missions. One experiment studied moonquakes. Another studied the moon's very thin atmosphere.

The astronauts also brought the Lunar Roving Vehicle (LRV). This four-wheeled vehicle looked a bit like a car. The astronauts drove it around. The LRV let them travel farther than they could by walking. They studied a wider area than previous astronauts. The astronauts stayed on the moon for three days. They brought 243 pounds (110 kg) of material back with them. They landed on Earth on December 19, 1972.

▲ Apollo 17 carried three astronauts to the moon.

GLOSSARY

astronauts (AS-troh-nots) Astronauts are people who go on missions in space. Some astronauts have walked on the moon.

atmosphere (AT-muss-feer) An atmosphere is the layer of gases that surrounds a planet. The moon has almost no atmosphere.

craters (KRAY-turz) Craters are large holes dug in the ground when rocks from space slam into a moon, planet, or dwarf planet. The moon is covered in many craters.

gravity (GRAV-i-tee) Gravity is the force that pulls objects together. Because the moon is smaller than Earth, it has weaker gravity.

orbits (OR-bits) Something orbits another object when it moves in a round path around that object. The moon orbits Earth.

rockets (ROK-its) Rockets are machines that launch things into space. Rockets have sent many missions to the moon.

spacecraft (SPAYSS-kraft) A spacecraft is a machine that is made to fly in space. People need a spacecraft to survive on the moon.

tides (TYDZ) Tides are the rise and fall of water in the ocean. The moon's gravity helps create tides on Earth.

TO LEARN MORE

IN THE LIBRARY

Hutchison, Patricia. *The First Moon Landing.* Mankato, MN: The Child's World, 2016.

Lapin, Joyce. *If You Had Your Birthday Party on the Moon.* New York, NY: Sterling Children's Books, 2019.

Nagelhout, Ryan. *20 Fun Facts about the Moon.* New York, NY: Gareth Stevens Publishing, 2015.

ON THE WEB

Visit our website for links about the moon:
childsworld.com/links

Note to Parents, Teachers, and Librarians: We routinely verify our Web links to make sure they are safe and active sites. So encourage your readers to check them out!

INDEX

Aldrin, Buzz, 19
Apollo 11, 19–21
appearance, 5–6, 12, 14
Armstrong, Neil, 19

Collins, Michael, 19
craters, 12, 13, 17

regolith, 14, 21

size, 8

tides, 9